POPULAR C...

A VIEW FROM THE PAPARAZZI

Orlando Bloom	John Legend
Kelly Clarkson	Lindsay Lohan
Johnny Depp	Mandy Moore
Hilary Duff	Ashlee and Jessica Simpson
Will Ferrell	
Jake Gyllenhaal	Justin Timberlake
Paris and Nicky Hilton	Owen and Luke Wilson
LeBron James	Tiger Woods

Ashlee and Jessica Simpson

Kristy Kaminsky and Brian Domboski

Mason Crest Publishers

Ashlee and Jessica Simpson

FRONTIS
Talented sisters Jessica and Ashlee Simpson each followed different paths to achieve stardom in the entertainment world.

Produced by 21st Century Publishing and Communications, Inc.

Copyright © 2008 by Mason Crest Publishers. All rights reserved. No part of this publication may be reproduced or transmitted in any form or by any means, electronic or mechanical, including photocopying, recording, taping, or any information storage and retrieval system, without permission from the publisher.

MASON CREST PUBLISHERS INC.
370 Reed Road
Broomall, Pennsylvania 19008
(866) MCP-BOOK (toll free)
www.masoncrest.com

Printed in the United States.

First Printing

9 8 7 6 5 4 3 2 1

Library of Congress Cataloging-in-Publication Data

Kaminsky, Kristy.
  Ashlee and Jessica Simpson / Kristy Kaminsky and Brian Domboski.
    p. cm. — (Pop culture: a view from the paparazzi)
  Includes bibliographical references and index.
  Hardback edition: ISBN-13: 978-1-4222-0208-1
  Paperback edition: ISBN-13: 978-1-4222-0363-7
  1. Simpson, Jessica, 1980– 2. Simpson, Ashlee. 3. Singers—United States—Biography—Juvenile literature. I. Domboski, Brian. II. Title.
ML3930.S57K36 2007
782.42164092'2—dc22
[B]   2007016481

Publisher's notes:
- All quotations in this book come from original sources, and contain the spelling and grammatical inconsistencies of the original text.

- The Web sites mentioned in this book were active at the time of publication. The publisher is not responsible for Web sites that have changed their addresses or discontinued operation since the date of publication. The publisher will review and update the Web site addresses each time the book is reprinted.

CONTENTS

1	**Superstar Sisters**	**7**
2	**A Family Affair**	**13**
3	**Newlyweds**	**23**
4	**The Downside of Fame**	**35**
5	**Lessons Learned**	**45**
	Chronology	**56**
	Accomplishments & Awards	**58**
	Further Reading & Internet Resources	**60**
	Glossary	**61**
	Index	**62**
	Picture Credits	**64**
	About the Author	**64**

CHAD & SOPHIA: WHAT WENT WRONG?

Teen People

ARTISTS OF THE YEAR AWARDS PG. 107

50 BEST GIFTS TO GIVE AND GET

HOLIDAY GLAM
Party-perfect dresses, shoes, hair & makeup

Sister Power!
HOW ASHLEE & JESSICA SIMPSON STUCK TOGETHER

The December 2005/January 2006 issue of *Teen People* was the first time Ashlee and Jessica Simpson appeared together on a magazine cover. The gifted sisters from Texas are among the most successful siblings in the history of pop music, and have been able to forge solid careers outside of the music industry.

1

Superstar Sisters

Ashlee and Jessica Simpson are among the most successful siblings in the history of pop music. Each has sold millions of albums, headlined successful tours, and appeared in popular music videos. And both Ashlee and Jessica have dabbled in other areas of entertainment and fashion, appearing in movies and on television shows and signing contracts to endorse various products.

The Simpson sisters are the constant targets of the **paparazzi**, with their every move photographed and reported on in celebrity gossip magazines like *People*, *US Weekly*, and *Star*. Fashion critics and the general public alike discuss the clothes, shoes, and accessories that they wear to major award shows, as well as the way they appear on trips to the supermarket.

Ashlee and Jessica Simpson first became famous in part from their appearances on **reality television** shows on MTV. These programs allowed viewers an intimate glimpse into their lives, from the inside story of how they wrote and recorded their songs to their everyday conversations with friends and family members. The exposure from the reality shows, music videos, movies, and albums have led to both sisters winning Teen Choice Awards and People's Choice Awards, along with other nominations and honors.

Long Road to Stardom

Despite the immediate and substantial impact of reality television on the careers of Jessica and Ashlee Simpson, they are no overnight sensations. The entire Simpson family, including their parents, Joe and Tina Simpson, and their grandmother, Joyce, all invested their time, effort, and money towards getting Jessica's and Ashlee's careers on track.

The Simpson sisters' path to stardom began in the early 1990s, when their parents recognized that the two girls were very talented. While Jessica carved out her **niche** as a Christian singer, Ashlee became the youngest student ever admitted to the prestigious School of American Ballet in New York City. Jessica eventually was signed to a **mainstream** pop record company and released two moderately successful albums. At the same time Ashlee started an acting career, eventually landing a recurring role on the family drama *7th Heaven*.

It was Jessica's starring role in the MTV reality show *Newlyweds: Nick and Jessica* that would propel the blonde singer to stardom. When the program first aired in August 2003 it was an immediate hit, and launched Jessica and her husband, pop singer Nick Lachey of the band 98 Degrees, to a new level of celebrity. Jessica's fame was ensured with the release of her third album, *In This Skin*, which eventually sold more than 4 million copies.

Soon after *Newlyweds* aired, Jessica spoke about making the program to *Redbook* magazine. "It's a weird adjustment to have cameras watching you," she told author Katherine Dykstra, adding:

"But we don't have anything to hide. It was actually best walking into the show blindly. We didn't have expectations. We wanted people to know how normal

Superstar Sisters 9

Jessica cuddles with her husband Nick Lachey, then a singer with the band 98 Degrees. Their MTV reality show *Newlyweds: Nick and Jessica* introduced the entertainers to a huge audience and helped to make both performers into huge stars. Thanks to the popularity of *Newlyweds*, fans wanted to know more about Jessica.

ASHLEE AND JESSICA SIMPSON

> we are—that we get frustrated dealing with newlywed things. We also felt that it was important for people to fall in love with us as a couple, because we are in love."

Many viewers did fall in love with Jessica and Nick. The success of *Newlyweds* also helped boost interest in Ashlee, and she was soon offered her own recording contract. Her debut album, *Autobiography*, was released in 2004 and immediately shot to the top of the music charts. Several of Ashlee's songs became hits, the biggest being "Pieces of Me."

Over the next few years, Jessica and Ashlee would branch out in other areas of entertainment. Each has appeared in major motion pictures as well as television programs and specials. Each has performed

Ashlee's debut album, *Autobiography*, was released in the summer of 2004. *Autobiography* contained several hit songs and was one of the bestselling albums of the year, reaching number one on the Billboard chart. Its success brought Ashlee out of her older sister's shadow, making her a star in her own right.

their songs or been interviewed on such highly rated programs as *The Tonight Show*, *Saturday Night Live*, and *Oprah*. In addition, the Simpson sisters are often hired to endorse products. They have appeared in commercials for such companies as Pizza Hut, Sketchers sneakers, and the acne medication Proactiv.

A Close Relationship

Throughout their rise to stardom, Jessica and Ashlee have remained close. They admit to a certain amount of competition, especially when both were younger. Ashlee consciously tried to set herself apart from her older sister by embarking on an acting career while Jessica was focused on music. When Ashlee began pursuing her own musical dream, she wore different clothing and performed a very different style of music than her sister had. But both supported each other. In an interview, Ashlee said:

> "We're sisters. . . . For us it's not about competition. If she succeeds, then I'm happy, and if I succeed, then our family wins no matter what."

Jessica has commented that she admires her younger sister and appreciates her support. She told *Teen People*:

> "I wish I could have some of [Ashlee's] personality traits. She's assertive; I mean, she moved to New York [for ballet school] when she was 11! I was still holding my mom's hand to cross the street! She's always been independent, and I've always been dependent."

Jessica and Ashlee have depended on each other for support, especially as their fame brought increased scrutiny by the media and paparazzi. With the glamorous sisters' every move scrutinized, their missteps became fodder for gossip magazines, Internet blogs, and public discussion. To deal with the pressure, Jessica and Ashlee had to rely on each other, their family, and their faith to pull them through. This is their story of determination and **perseverance** in achieving their dreams and how they have dealt with the attention as they work to stay on top.

The Simpson family attends the premiere of Jessica's movie *The Dukes of Hazzard* in Los Angeles, July 2005. Pictured are (left to right) Ashlee and Jessica's father Joe Simpson, Jessica, Nick Lachey, mother Tina Simpson, and Ashlee. The sisters have attributed their success to their parents' strong influence and moral values.

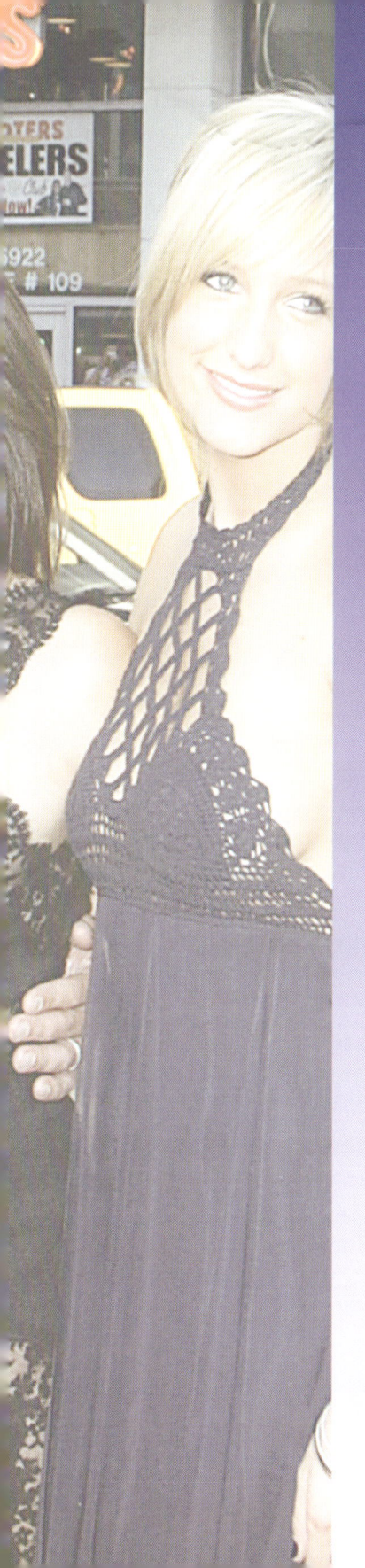

2
A Family Affair

Jessica and Ashlee have attributed much of their success to their close-knit family, and in particular the strong morals and values instilled in them by their parents. Despite the fame and fortune brought by their television and music success, the sisters have made an effort to remain true to those values and close to their family.

Their parents, Joe Truett Simpson and Tina Ann Drew, had married and moved to Abilene, Texas, to start their family. Their first child, Jessica Ann, was born on July 10, 1980. Jessica's sister, Ashlee Nicole, was born on October 3, 1984.

The two sisters were close from an early age. Tina Simpson remembers one time when Ashlee was a newborn, she could not find Jessica after putting baby Ashlee to sleep. After searching the entire house, Tina went back into Ashlee's room, where she found Jessica sleeping under the crib.

The girls' father, Joe Simpson, was a therapist and Baptist minister at Heights Baptist Church in Richardson, Texas. He instilled in his daughters a strong faith in God and stressed the importance of family. Jessica later told *GQ* magazine:

> "My father was also a little **secular** for the Bible world. He wanted to bring young people in, so he'd take everybody paint balling, take everybody to dances; girls could wear bikinis at summer camp or whatever.... I was definitely the opposite of whatever most people think a preacher's daughter is, the wild child."

A Career in Music

The church was an integral part of both girls' upbringings, and was the place where Jessica and Ashlee were first exposed to music. Both girls began singing hymns in the church choir when they were young.

Jessica's parents recognized that she was a talented singer. When she was 12 years old, they allowed her to audition to join the cast of a new Disney television program, *The All-New Mickey Mouse Club*. Jessica was among the young performers who made it to the final round, but she was not selected. Among those young people who did appear on the show were several future pop stars, including Justin Timberlake, Christina Aguilera, and Britney Spears.

Despite this setback Joe and Tina believed Jessica could be a star, and they encouraged her to continue following her dream of becoming an entertainer. On weekends and during summers, Jessica sang **contemporary** Christian music at local churches, camps, and festivals. When she was in high school, the head of a small Christian record label, Proclaim Records, offered Jessica a recording contract. She continued to attend J.J. Pearce High School while she recorded her first album. Unfortunately, the label went out of business before the album was finished and released.

A Family Affair

Ashlee (left) and Jessica in a photo from their childhood. The girls were very close growing up. From an early age, both Ashlee and Jessica were interested in performing. "I did dance classes, went on to dance competitions—that's what I did as a little kid," Jessica later commented. "I was definitely into the whole performance thing."

Dancing Difficulties

During this time, Ashlee Simpson was also beginning to make her way in the world of performing arts. Unlike her older sister, Ashlee's focus was on dancing rather than singing. Ashlee had started dancing when she was four years old. When she was 11, she became the youngest student ever granted admission into the prestigious School of American Ballet in New York City.

The practice, training, and competition at the School of American Ballet was hard on Ashlee. She had to deal with self-image issues that eventually contributed to her suffering from an eating disorder, **anorexia nervosa**. In the January 2006 issue of *Cosmopolitan* magazine, Ashlee spoke frankly about her troubles:

> "It was about six months of not eating too much at all. . . . I was 11 and 5 feet 2 and about 70 pounds."

With the support of her family, Ashlee was able to overcome her problems and learn to accept herself for who she was. She spent the next three years studying at the prestigious school.

Promoting Jessica

Jessica, who had been a cheerleader and the homecoming queen in her high school, was allowed to drop out of school in her senior year so she could promote her demo album. Her grandmother Joyce had paid to have the album created, showing how important family support was early in Jessica's career.

Joe's job as a minister began to take a backseat to managing and promoting young Jessica on the Christian Youth Conference circuit. She performed throughout Texas and the southern United States, at times sharing the stage with such well-known gospel singers as Kirk Franklin and CeCe Wynanns. After performances, they met with Christian music fans, posed for pictures, signed autographs, and sold copies of her CD.

Despite being blessed with an obvious talent for singing, and a strong devotion to Christian values, Jessica met some resistance as she sought another record deal. Some talent scouts and representatives of Christian record labels were wary about Jessica. Even though Jessica had spent much of her life singing God's praises in song, they felt her physical beauty did not mesh well with the Christian ideals they wanted to promote in their artists.

After being turned down numerous times, Jessica started to think about giving up her dream. However, everything changed when Tommy Mottola, an executive at the enormous entertainment **conglomerate** Sony Music, heard her demo album. Mottola had helped to launch the careers of such talented singers as Mariah Carrey, Celine Dion, Destiny's Child, and Shakira. He felt Jessica had great potential as a pop singer, and offered her a recording contract with Columbia Records.

A Family Affair   17

Jessica performs during halftime at a Dallas Cowboys football game, November 2000. Although she started out singing on the Christian music circuit, her career did not take off until Sony Music executive Tommy Mottola "discovered" her in 1999 and signed her to Columbia Records. Jessica's first single, "I Wanna Love You Forever," was a major hit.

From Gospel to Pop

To build a fan base for Jessica, the record label sent her out on tour. She was the opening act for the band 98 Degrees, and performed more than 60 shows to build a fan base prior to the release of her first album. She later told Yahoo Music:

> "[E]verybody just screams the whole time. I mean, it's nonstop screaming. We thought we were going to go deaf by the end of the tour.... But I loved opening up for 98 Degrees because it was fun.... Their fans are fun."

In September 1999, Jessica's first single, "I Wanna Love You Forever," was released by Columbia. The song was a major hit, reaching number three on the Billboard Hot 100. Thanks to the success of the song, the record label hurried to complete Jessica's first album. *Sweet Kisses* was released later in 1999.

Jessica's second single from *Sweet Kisses*, "Where You Are," was a duet with Nick Lachey, a singer with 98 Degrees. It was only a minor hit when it was released in early 2000. The third single from the album, "I Think I'm in Love," was more successful, reaching number 12 on the Billboard Top 40 chart in the United States.

Although *Sweet Kisses* eventually sold over 2 million copies, it was not quite as successful as albums by two other young female singers with whom Jessica was often compared, Britney Spears and Christina Aguilera. Britney's debut album had sold more than 15 million copies, while Christina's first record had sold over 8 million copies. Although *Sweet Kisses* was not in their league with regard to sales, the album did net Jessica her first two Teen Choice Awards, for Choice Breakout Artist and Love Song of the Year (for "Where You Are").

Thanks to her growing popularity, Jessica appeared at the 2000 Christmas Special in Washington, D.C., and performed at the presidential inauguration of fellow Texan George W. Bush in January 2001.

Changing Strategy

To follow up on the success of *Sweet Kisses*, Jessica soon began working on her second album. In 2001, Columbia released *Irresistible*. For a few weeks the record sold very well, reaching number six on Billboard's chart of bestselling albums. However, sales soon tailed off, and overall *Irresistible*'s sales of about 800,000 copies were a disappointment.

A Family Affair 19

Two singles were released. The first, "Irresistible," was a big hit that reached number 15 on the Billboard chart. The second single, "A Little Bit," did not chart in the United States.

Some people speculated that Jessica's squeaky-clean image was one reason sales of her records lagged behind those of Britney and Christina. Both had flaunted their sexuality in their songs and videos. Jessica's management team soon began to change its strategy.

Thanks to the success of her first single, Columbia decided to release an album of Jessica's music. *Sweet Kisses* was released in 1999 and eventually sold more than 2 million copies. According to a review of the album in *Billboard* magazine, "the lovely Simpson . . . has the soulful pipes to go the platinum distance."

ASHLEE AND JESSICA SIMPSON

While Jessica was pursuing a career as a pop singer, Ashlee was taking a different route to fame. She found acting work on several television shows before landing a steady job on the TV drama *7th Heaven*. Despite this success Ashlee still maintained her own dream of becoming a singing star.

In January 2002 Jessica posed in lingerie for the men's magazine *Maxim*, and she was subsequently named to the top spot in the publication's annual list of 100 sexy women.

The change didn't help sales of her next album, *This Is the Remix*, a compilation of new versions of some of her old hits. The album only sold about 500,000 copies worldwide.

Ashlee's Career Takes Off

While Jessica aggressively pursued her music career, her sister Ashlee chose a different route to fame. When Jessica received her Columbia Records contract, the Simpson family moved to Los Angeles. While there, Ashlee was hired to appear in several television commercials. As Jessica's career took off, Ashlee joined her on tour as a background dancer.

Ashlee soon began to emerge from her older sister's shadow. Her first significant acting job was an appearance as a major character's girlfriend on an episode of the Fox sitcom *Malcolm in the Middle* during 2001. That led to a small role in the 2002 feature film *The Hot Chick*, as a friend of the main character.

Ashlee's next acting job was more permanent. She was hired for a recurring role on the popular television drama *7th Heaven*. Over two seasons in 2002 and 2003, Ashlee appeared in 39 episodes of the program, playing the part of Cecilia Smith, the girlfriend of young Simon Camden.

Although Ashlee enjoyed the chance to act on a steady basis, she still had dreams of following her sister into a successful music career. She later told MTV.com:

> "I've been singing since I was young, but I didn't always know that I could really sing—I kind of always thought that was Jessica's thing and that I was supposed to do something else. Then, I started writing my own music and finally decided that I really liked my songs, and that I could do it too!"

In mid-2003 television exposure on another pair of popular shows would give Ashlee the opportunity to chase her own musical **aspirations**, and would propel Jessica from middling pop singer to pop culture superstar.

A promotional photo from *Newlyweds: Nick and Jessica*, which first aired in August 2003 on MTV. Jessica's naïve comments and her sweet nature created her image as a bubbly blonde airhead that Americans could not help but love. The show was a huge hit and attracted millions of viewers each week.

3

Newlyweds

With cameras whirring, Jessica Simpson entered the living room wearing a pair of dark sweatpants and one of her husband Nick Lachey's oversized T-shirts. Nick had just settled onto their plush couch to watch a basketball game on television in their beautiful Calabasas, California, mansion. Holding a bowl of tuna fish, Jessica plopped down beside Nick and asked:

> "Is this chicken, what I have, or is this fish? I know it's tuna. But it says 'chicken.' By the sea. Is that stupid?"

Nick gave Jessica a long double take, shook his head slowly, then patiently explained how they had eaten tuna just like this on many occasions, and that it was in fact, fish. The brand was called "Chicken of the Sea" because it was eaten so commonly, much like chicken. His answer seemed to satisfy her, as she said she had "read it wrong" on the can.

With that brief conversation broadcast for the world to see on August 19, 2003, Nick Lachey and his wife of three months, Jessica Simpson, became America's newest reality show stars. Some 2.5 million people watched that episode of their MTV show *Newlyweds: Nick and Jessica*. The program would become one of the most popular programs on the network and would help both Jessica and Ashlee to become major stars.

Romance on the Rise

Jessica Simpson had first met Nick Lachey at a Hollywood Christmas party in 1998. About a month later they met again at a party sponsored by the magazine *Teen People*. Their interest in each other was evident, and at the end of that night Nick called his mother and told her that one day he would marry Jessica.

The two dated during 1999, when Jessica was working as the opening act for 98 Degrees. In a video for the group's hit song "My Everything," she played Nick's love interest. Nick returned the favor by recording a duet with Jessica on her first album.

As a celebrity couple, Nick and Jessica were always in the public eye. That pressure may have caused them to break up briefly during 2001. However, they rekindled their relationship after the tragic terrorist attacks on New York City and Washington, D.C., on September 11, 2001. Nick and his band had been planning to fly out of New York that day, and Jessica was frantic when she heard the news that airplanes had been hijacked and crashed into the World Trade Center. Later, she told the Associated Press:

> "After 9/11, I knew that I never ever wanted to be away from Nick ever for the rest of my life."

A Wedding Proposal

Because Nick is a big sports fan, in February 2002 Nick and Jessica traveled to Hawaii for the NFL Pro Bowl. Nick chartered a boat, and just as the sun hit the perfect spot on the horizon, he asked Jessica to marry him. Jessica, of course, said yes, later telling *People* magazine,

Newlyweds

> **"I was wearing a huge sweatshirt that came down to my knees. If I'd known he was going to propose, I would have at least dressed cute."**

The couple generated significant media attention as they planned their wedding. Jessica publicly announced that she was a virgin, and would remain one until her wedding night. She also began writing a book about wedding planning.

After Jessica's famous "chicken or fish" moment, the singer was invited to visit the tuna canning company Chicken of the Sea, where she signed autographs and toured the facility. The media covered the visit heavily, with 10 national television shows and 22 cable shows broadcasting clips—an indication of how popular Jessica had become.

ASHLEE AND JESSICA SIMPSON

teen VOGUE

special issue
FALL 2000

Pop's New Princess
JESSICA SIMPSON
platinum hits, superstar style & Nick too!

fall fashion
LOOKS YOU HAVE TO HAVE

THE END OF ACNE
A Magic Pill?

great jeans

Even before *Newlyweds* made Nick and Jessica into huge celebrities, their romance was the subject of stories and reports in many magazines, such as *Teen Vogue*'s Fall 2000 issue. Although they broke up in April 2001, after the September 11 terrorist attacks on the United States they got back together. Nick proposed to Jessica in February 2002.

The wedding took place in Austin, Texas on October 26, 2002. Some 350 family members and friends joined Jessica and Nick for the celebration, and it was covered by *InStyle* magazine. Jessica walked down the aisle in a strapless gown covered in pearls that was made by renowned designer Vera Wang. During the couple's wedding reception, the members of 98 Degrees sang "My Everything" to Jessica, with Nick becoming emotional and teary-eyed while singing to his new wife. Camera crews documented their whole wedding and continued recording their first few months of marriage. Much of this footage would later be included in the reality series that MTV was developing.

Nick and Jessica on Camera

In the late 1990s, reality shows like *Survivor* and *Fear Factor* were becoming more common and popular. Typically, these **unscripted** shows featured ordinary people performing stunts or competing against each other in various contests. Television networks liked reality shows not only because they drew high ratings, but also because the cost to produce them was much lower than the cost of a typical half-hour sitcom or drama.

Joe Simpson, Jessica's father and manager, had approached MTV with the idea for a show about Nick and Jessica in 2002. He figured that if large numbers of viewers would tune in to see regular people in unscripted situations, they would be interested in the private lives of their favorite celebrities as well. MTV soon gave the program a green light.

Newlyweds: Nick and Jessica allowed viewers an intimate glimpse into the personal lives of the two pop stars. It showed everything from the couple preparing dinner to Jessica finding backup dancers for her upcoming tour. The show allowed viewers to see these famous pop stars as real people, letting viewers eavesdrop on their everyday conversations.

While the show was supposed to show their real lives and personalities, careful editing allowed producers to assign roles and dominating characteristics to both of the main characters. Jessica was portrayed as a doe-eyed, air-headed ditz. At one point she declined an order of buffalo chicken wings, saying that she "doesn't eat buffalo." Another time, she created the **malapropism** "ventures," when she incorrectly combined the words "veneers" and "dentures." *Rolling Stone* magazine described Nick as an "eye-rolling everyman."

Superstars

The show was a pleasant surprise to executives at MTV, as it maintained surprisingly high ratings, averaging 1.4 million viewers throughout its entire four-season run. It also helped turn the couple into pop culture personalities and had a great impact on Jessica's record sales.

Columbia decided to release Jessica's fourth album, *In This Skin*, in August 2003, around the same time that *Newlyweds* premiered. The album initially debuted at number 10, but soon dropped off the Billboard charts. However, sales gradually improved during the holiday season, and it was re-released in 2004 with bonus tracks and a DVD. *In This Skin* would eventually be Jessica's best-selling album, with more than 4 million copies sold in the United States. Three singles from *In This Skin* were top-40 hits: "Sweetest Sin," "With You," and "Take My Breath Away."

The show was not quite as helpful for Nick, who released his first solo album, *SoulO*, in November 2003. Despite heavy advertising by the record company, *SoulO* was a flop. Nick later told *Rolling Stone* that he felt his label had not used the *Newlyweds* show to promote his music properly. He said:

> "Jessica's label did this really smart thing and tied her next single into the show. My label didn't. So my record stagnated."

Despite this disappointment, Nick and Jessica remained in demand. On Easter Sunday 2004 they starred in a television special, *The Nick and Jessica Variety Hour*. The show was filled with comedy, singing, and a variety of guests including Jewel, Mr. T, Kermit the Frog and Miss Piggy, Kenneth "Babyface" Edmonds, and Kenny Rogers. Jessica sang a duet with Jewel, while Nick sang a Stevie Wonder song with Babyface.

In the fall of 2004 Jessica released an album of traditional holiday music, called *Rejoyce: The Christmas Album*. The record's title honors her grandmother Joyce, who supported Jessica in the early part of her career. *Rejoyce* included duets with Ashlee (on the song "Little Drummer Boy,") and Nick (on "Baby It's Cold Outside"). The record quickly sold over 500,000 copies, which was a good showing for a Christmas album.

Ashlee's Big Break

In addition to making Nick and Jessica "A-List" celebrities, the show also introduced viewers to some of their family members, including

Newlyweds

Nick and Jessica sign autographs for fans. Although both had been stars before *Newlyweds*, the show propelled them to a new level of celebrity. *Newlyweds* producer Rod Aissa explained the show's appeal: "The twist to this show is that while Jessica and Nick are stars, they're also real people who have to experience the dynamics of a real relationship."

Joe Simpson and Nick's brother Drew. For Ashlee Simpson, the show offered a platform from which she could follow her dreams of becoming a recording artist.

Viewers of *Newlyweds* could see that Ashlee had a very different personality and style than her older sister. Where Jessica was a sweet

ASHLEE AND JESSICA SIMPSON

Although Nick's 2003 album *SoulO* did not benefit from the popularity of *Newlyweds*, Jessica and Nick remained in great demand. Here they are photographed at a party after the American Music Awards ceremony in Los Angeles with legendary music industry executive Clive Davis, record producer Jermaine Dupri, and singer Janet Jackson.

pop star, Ashlee preferred a harder-edged punk rock style. Ashlee had already recorded one song, "Just Let Me Cry," which had appeared on the soundtrack for the 2003 film *Freaky Friday*. Her appearances on *Newlyweds* led to a recording contract with Geffen Records.

Ashlee also agreed to appear on a new MTV reality show, which would air in the time slot after *Newlyweds*. *The Ashlee Simpson Show* followed the same formula as *Newlyweds*, giving viewers an intimate glimpse into the business and personal life of its subject. Ashlee later spoke about the experience with MSNBC:

Newlyweds

> **"I wasn't that wild about having the cameras in my face, but my dad thought it would be a good way for everyone to get to know me as me, and not as Jessica's little sister. . . . Our personalities are so different it reflects in our music."**

The first season of *The Ashlee Simpson Show* aired during the summer of 2004. Episodes documented how she wrote songs and showed Ashlee recording her first Geffen album, *Autobiography*. It also showed her interacting with some of her boyfriends, including actor Josh Henderson and singer Ryan Cabrera.

When Ashlee emerged on the music scene, she exhibited a very different personality and style than her older sister. Where Jessica was known for straightforward pop love songs, Ashlee tended toward introspective songs with a harder, rock music edge. She wrote most of the songs on her debut album, *Autobiography*.

ASHLEE AND JESSICA SIMPSON

Ashlee's MTV reality show helped create buzz for the release of her debut album. Many music critics appreciated the album, comparing her to rockers like Avril Lavigne and Courtney Love. "[Ashlee's] *Autobiography* is packed with insidiously catchy songs, especially the first single, 'Pieces of Me,'" wrote a reviewer in *Entertainment Weekly*.

A Hit Record

Thanks to Ashlee's hard work, and the invaluable exposure of her show, *Autobiography* debuted at number one on the Billboard Hot 100 chart in July 2004, something that Jessica's albums had never done. *Autobiography* sold nearly 400,000 copies in the first week, and eventually sold more than 6 million copies.

Ashlee's personal feelings spilled over into her songs—the top-five hit "Pieces of Me" was inspired by Cabrera, "Unreachable" spoke of Josh Henderson, and the successful single "Shadow" was about growing up in the shadow of her older sister Jessica. Ashlee later explained that for her, writing the songs was like writing a diary, saying:

> "My inspiration came from what I have gone through in the past three years. Every single day I was thinking of what I was going through and would write songs about it."

Critical response to *Autobiography* was mixed. *People* magazine called the album a "passable debut" and noted that Ashlee was a "credible talent in her own right." However, *Rolling Stone* called the album "mundane" and described Ashlee's singing as "wailing in lieu of hitting notes." With such a mixed response, Ashlee claimed to be surprised by *Autobiography*'s success. She told *Seventeen* magazine:

> "I just hoped my album charted. I didn't expect it to be number one in the country! It was a huge shock."

By the fall of 2004, both Jessica and Ashlee Simpson were riding a huge wave of popularity. Both had established themselves as very popular recording stars and television personalities. However, over the next few years both of the Simpson sisters would experience heartbreaking lows as well as soaring successes.

Ashlee and Jessica pose for a photo after the 2004 Video Music Awards in Miami. Although the two talented sisters enjoyed their fame, they soon found that constant media attention had a downside. During 2004 and 2005 Jessica and Ashlee each experienced turbulent moments in their careers and personal lives.

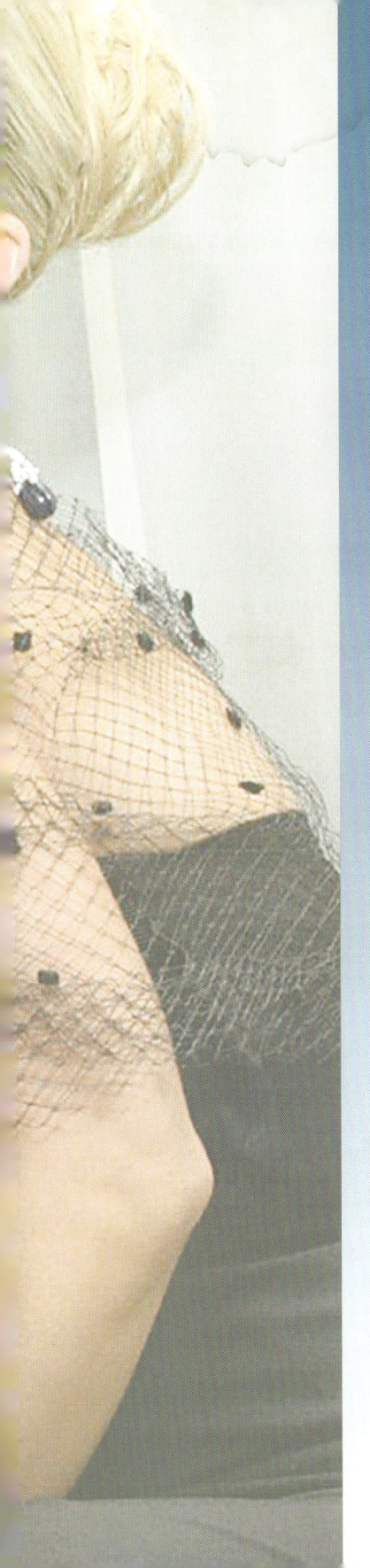

4
The Downside of Fame

There is no question that the careers and lives of Jessica and Ashlee Simpson were boosted by their appearances on reality television. The widespread media exposure brought the Simpson sisters greater fame than they could have ever imagined. The perks were obvious: their prominence enabled them to become rich from record sales and endorsement deals.

But Jessica and Ashlee soon found out that there is a downside to celebrity. Life in the public eye provides little privacy, and any mistake that either one made soon became a cover story for national gossip magazines. Their clothes, hairstyles, and behavior were dissected on a weekly basis, and many times the critics were not favorable. Nick and Jessica have said that the constant presence of cameras in their lives introduced many difficulties into their marriage. In 2005 Jessica told *Teen People*:

> "It gets to the point where it's so frustrating that you just want to get away. I almost flipped my Range Rover trying to get away from the paparazzi. . . . But Nick and I have been so public [about our marriage] that it made people obsessed. We set ourselves up to be gawked at."

Backing Track Backlash

At first, Ashlee did not intend to do a second season of her reality show. In September 2004 she told *Blender* magazine, "Jessica may be happy having cameras in her life 24/7, but not me. It's not natural." She changed her mind the next month, perhaps because of the success of the first season and of her album.

The second season of *The Ashlee Simpson Show* focused on her life from October 2004 through February 2005, when she moved into her own house and began preparations for a headlining tour to support the album. The first episode included preparations for her upcoming performances as a musical guest on *Saturday Night Live* on October 23, 2004.

On *Saturday Night Live*, Ashlee was scheduled to sing two songs from *Autobiography*, her hit "Pieces of Me" and the title track, "Autobiography." Her first performance went off without a hitch, but the second one turned out to be a disaster. When the band began playing "Autobiography," the vocals to "Pieces of Me" could be heard loud and clear before Ashlee had even put the microphone to her mouth to begin singing.

Ashlee was clearly rattled. She did an awkward dance, then walked off the stage without saying a word, leaving her band to continue playing the song for nearly a full minute before *Saturday Night Live* cut to a commercial. At the end of the show, Ashlee apologized, saying that that the band had played the wrong song. However, her critics saw the incident as evidence that she was lip synching. They claimed that this was a sign Ashlee was little more than a manufactured studio creation, rather than a true artist.

The Downside of Fame

Ashlee belts out a song in a recording studio, 2004. Many people's opinions about Ashlee changed practically overnight after her embarrassing appearance on *Saturday Night Live* in October 2004, when it appeared that she was lip-synching during the live broadcast. Critics believed that studio tricks, rather than her own singing talent, were responsible for her success.

Trying to Explain

On Monday afternoon following the incident, Ashlee called MTV's *Total Request Live* to explain her side of the story. She said that she had been suffering from severe **acid reflux disease**, which had caused problems with her voice. To help her performance, she had been told to sing along to a pre-recorded vocal guide track. When the song "Autobiography" started, the drummer had hit the wrong button, starting the wrong guide track. She admitted to feeling very embarrassed about making a fool of herself on *Saturday Night Live*.

38 ASHLEE AND JESSICA SIMPSON

Despite her humiliation at the lip-synching accusations, Ashlee's career did not suffer permanent damage. Six weeks later she was named Best New Artist at the 2004 Billboard Music Awards, and she completed a very successful tour to support *Autobiography*. Her second album, *I Am Me*, was released in the fall of 2005 and proved to be another hit.

The next week, video of Ashlee filmed during a rehearsal for the show aired on *60 Minutes*. It supported her claim that she was having trouble with her voice, showing the young singer upset. Despite this, Ashlee became a national punch line, as comedians and late-night television hosts cracked many jokes at her expense. Online petitions were circulated asking for Ashlee to stop recording and performing.

Ashlee's next major public appearance, a halftime performance at the Orange Bowl in January 2005, was another disaster. She sang her third single from *Autobiography*, "La La," but was booed relentlessly at the end of her show. Some people thought the booing was backlash from the *Saturday Night Live* appearance. Others said that her voice had been out of tune. Ashlee downplayed the booing and criticism, saying:

> "If they didn't like the performance, and that's what it was about, then sorry to them. Maybe they were booing at me, maybe they were booing at the halftime show 'cause the whole thing sucked. I was facing [the Oklahoma Sooners], and I was rooting for USC, and they played a clip of it, so maybe it was that those people didn't like me. You never know. But I can't make everybody happy."

Despite the adversity Ashlee pressed on with her tour, and it ultimately proved to be very successful. In October 2005 she released her second album, *I Am Me*, which like her first album, debuted at the top of the Billboard charts and went **platinum** within two months. The album addressed many of her issues since the initial controversy. When she made a second visit to *Saturday Night Live*, she performed the song "Catch Me When I Fall," which spoke directly about the backing track incident. The success of her second album and continued support of her fans seemed to indicate that Ashlee had weathered the storm.

Constant Scrutiny

Like Ashlee, Jessica was also under a media microscope during 2004 and 2005. She continued to film episodes of *Newlyweds* with Nick, but the constant presence of cameras made their personal lives very difficult. In addition, while Nick and Jessica tried to remain true to themselves, the way the series was edited almost forced them to play caricatures of themselves. In a *Rolling Stone* interview, Nick admitted:

> **"Jessica and I began playing these parts even when we were by ourselves. It became a really blurred line. There was a question about what truly was our reality. When you are on a reality show, your life ceases to be reality. It becomes TV."**

Both Nick and Jessica were relieved when the last episode of *Newlyweds* aired in March 2005. The show had lasted for four very successful seasons, but they were ready to move on.

The end of *Newlyweds* did not mark the end of Nick and Jessica's privacy issues, however. Throughout 2005, gossip columns began predicting the collapse of their marriage. Rumors flew wildly when Jessica was photographed without her wedding ring, despite denials by both Nick and Jessica that anything was wrong. Joe Simpson even told the newspapers that the marriage was strong. Still, rumors of trouble in the marriage continued to emerge regularly in the pages of *US Weekly*, *People*, *Star*, and other publications. Nick later told *Rolling Stone*:

> **"All that stuff in the press—this week they split, this week they're back together. All that stuff was not our reality. Or I should say, it wasn't my reality. I wasn't trying to defend myself in the press. I was trying to defend my marriage to my spouse."**

A Starring Role

With the fame and media attention lavished on Jessica came greater opportunities within the entertainment world, including offers for roles in major motion pictures. Her first big film role was playing Daisy Duke in *The Dukes of Hazzard*, which began filming in 2004 in California. The movie was based on a television series that had been very popular in the early 1980s. Jessica's character, Daisy Duke, is a young waitress who dresses in sexy clothes; her cousins are the lead characters, Bo and Luke Duke.

When *The Dukes of Hazzard* was released in August 2005, it was an immediate hit. It was the number one film in its first week in theaters, and eventually earned more than $110 million at the box office. Movie critics did not like the film, with some calling it the worst movie of the year, and most writers criticized Jessica's acting. However, she did win a Teen Choice Award as Choice Breakout Female for her role

The Downside of Fame

"America's best-loved housewife Jessica Simpson amply fills out her Daisy Dukes in this big-screen remake of the TV series," wrote an *Interview* magazine reviewer about *The Dukes of Hazzard*. Jessica (third from right) was joined by an all-star cast that included (left to right) M.C. Rainey, Burt Reynolds, Willie Nelson, Seann William Scott, and Johnny Knoxville.

in the film. She was also nominated for two MTV Movie Awards: Best On-Screen Team (with costars Johnny Knoxville and Seann William Scott) and Sexiest Performance.

In addition to being one of the film's stars, Jessica contributed a song to the film's soundtrack. "These Boots Are Made for Walkin'" was a remake of a 1960s hit, although the words were changed to reflect Daisy Duke's perspective. The song was a hit for Jessica, reaching number 14 on the Billboard Hot 100 chart. She also made a controversial video to promote the song. In the video Jessica wears a sexy bikini and dances provocatively, causing some people to complain that she had completely abandoned her "good girl" image and Christian values.

ASHLEE AND JESSICA SIMPSON

ASHTON BEGS DEMI: NO MORE PLASTIC SURGERY!

Star — Breaking Celebrity News First!

THE OTHER WOMAN TELLS ALL!

WORLD EXCLUSIVE PHOTOS

NICK BUSTED WITH OTHER WOMAN!

Will This 19-Year-Old College Student End His

PARIS STEALS MARY-KATE'S

OCTOBER 17, 2005
$3.49 US / $4.79 Canada

Tabloid reports like this one helped cause the collapse of Nick and Jessica's marriage. "There wasn't one event that brought it about," a friend of Nick's told *People* in 2005. "I think it was a general growing apart, as in most marriages. It's very rare that it's just one thing that causes people to break up."

The Marriage Ends

Unfortunately, rumors soon circulated that Jessica had cheated on Nick with one of her costars, Johnny Knoxville, while making *The Dukes of Hazzard*. Although both denied that anything had happened, the rumors persisted. Soon, other rumors liked Jessica romantically to Bam Margera, a friend of Johnny Knoxville's; Maroon 5 lead singer Adam Levine; and Fred Durst of Limp Bizkit. Nick later spoke about how these rumors affected their marriage:

> "People forget we're real people dealing with real hurt. This wasn't some publicity stunt. This wasn't some scripted-for-reality-television romantic tragedy. . . . If you allow those things to enter into your life they will [mess] with you."

Finally, on Thanksgiving weekend in 2005, Nick and Jessica announced that they were separating. In December 2005, Jessica filed for divorce. Instead of ending the persistent media attention, the separation announcement and divorce process only fueled the gossip. Comedians had a field day when it was leaked that Nick had filed for spousal support. When the couple had married in 2002, Nick was the more successful partner. By 2006, Jessica was earning more money than Nick, who was publicly mocked for filing his claim for support. Their divorce was finalized in June 2006.

Because of the rumors of cheating, many people felt Jessica had caused the marriage to break up. As a result her popularity took a hit. One trendy store in Hollywood began selling "Team Nick" and "Team Jessica" shirts, and a newspaper gossip columnist reported that Jessica became upset when she saw a large stack of "Team Jessica" shirts next to a small stack of "Team Nick" shirts, indicating that the public supported Nick rather than her. For his part, Nick refused to wage a war of words in the magazines, saying:

> "Jessica being cast as the villain is unfair to her. Marriage is the toughest thing in the world—to blame her is [wrong]. The tabloids are carrying on the show. I know people want to know how the story is going to end."

Jessica and Ashlee pause for photographs at an awards show. Thanks in part to their close relationship, Ashlee and Jessica have learned how to handle the pressures of fame and enjoy their celebrity status. When one sister experiences turmoil in her personal or professional life, the other always steps in to offer support and advice.

5

Lessons Learned

Despite the perks that come with being beautiful, famous, and wealthy, the Simpson sisters have had to learn from their mistakes how to deal with the constant attention of the media. While both Jessica and Ashlee have made missteps along the way, each has been able to bounce back and enjoy the benefits of her fame.

More Controversy for Ashlee

Like Jessica, Ashlee has had to deal with the embarrassment of constant media scrutiny. In August 2005 her film *Undiscovered*, in which she played one of the leading parts, was a flop at the box office. Later that year, she became involved in a "celebrity feud" with actress and pop singer Lindsay Lohan. Gossip magazines reported that in the fall of 2004 Ashlee had secretly become romantically involved with Lohan's boyfriend, actor Wilmer Valderrama, a star of the sitcom *That '70's Show*. Lohan fumed and snubbed Ashlee at public events. Many people thought the song "Boyfriend" from the *I Am Me* album addressed the feud, but Ashlee claimed differently on MTV, saying:

> "[The song] is about [how] every girl out there sometimes thinks you stole her boyfriend. It's just making fun of that."

A more embarrassing problem emerged in November 2005, just a month after the release of *I Am Me*, when a video clip of Ashlee in a McDonald's restaurant appeared on the Internet. In the video Ashlee appears to be drunk. She argues with restaurant employees, eventually climbing up onto the counter and telling a fan to "kiss her feet" if he wanted an autograph. The episode prompted another wave of bad press for Ashlee. She later admitted that the incident served as a wake-up call that she needed to grow up.

Another controversy involving Ashlee occurred in March 2006, when she was interviewed in *Marie Claire* magazine. During the interview she said that Hollywood has a "twisted view of feminine beauty." She spoke about her problems with the eating disorder anorexia nervosa, and the lessons she had learned from it, commenting:

> "Everyone is made differently, and that's what makes us beautiful and 86.3% unique. I want girls to look in the mirror and feel confident."

However, by the time the issue hit the newsstands, it was clear that Ashlee had undergone cosmetic surgery to change the shape of her nose. She had also lightened her hair color and changed her clothing style to a more feminine-preppy look. Angry readers flooded the editors at *Marie Claire* with more than a thousand letters calling Ashlee a "hypocrite."

New Album, New Movie

With the breakup of her marriage to Nick, Jessica decided that she was ready for some changes. In 2006 she left Columbia and signed a new

Lessons Learned

A scene from *Undiscovered*, the 2005 film in which Ashlee played an aspiring actress and singer named Clea. Unfortunately, the movie received poor reviews and was a box-office flop. "Simpson steals the show—which, admittedly, isn't saying much considering her stiffest competition comes by way of a skateboarding bulldog," wrote film critic Kimberly Jones in the *Austin Chronicle*.

deal with Epic Records. Her first album with Epic, *A Public Affair*, was released in August. It debuted at number five on the Billboard charts, and was eventually certified as a gold record. Some of the songs on *A Public Affair* addressed the end of the marriage and her hopes for the future.

Overall, the songs on *A Public Affair* are sexier than Jessica's earlier work. She wrote all but one song on the album. The title track,

48 ASHLEE AND JESSICA SIMPSON

Paris Hilton, Lindsay Lohan, and Ashlee Simpson are photographed leaving a party. In late 2005 tabloids began reporting that Lindsay was angry at Ashlee for stealing her boyfriend, and that the actress was feuding with Jessica as well. However, all three denied that there was any substance to the tabloid stories.

"A Public Affair," was the album's first single; it was a number-one hit on Billboard's Dance Club chart and reached number 14 on the Hot 100. A video for the song featured cameos by several celebrities, including Eva Longoria, Christina Applegate, Andy Dick, and Ryan Seacrest. Two other singles, "I Belong to Me" and "You Spin Me 'Round (Like a Record)," were also released.

Billboard magazine music critic Chuck Taylor had good things to say about Jessica's album:

> "Giddy, wildly adventurous production from Lester Mendez is an absolute delight—maddeningly catchy and brimming with melodic twists and turns—giving "A Public Affair" the potential to actually signal a tidal shift back to the center for top 40—it's that good. . . . This record is perfect."

Also in 2006 Jessica was paid $1 million for her second starring film role. In the movie *Employee of the Month* she plays a beautiful cashier at a large discount store. Two other workers at the store, played by Dane Cook and Dax Shepard, complete to win the "employee of the month" award in order to get her attention. The movie was released in October, and soon became profitable, eventually earning about $30 million. It was released on DVD in January 2007.

In December 2006 Jessica had her own "Ashlee moment," flubbing the lyrics to the song "9 to 5" during a tribute to Dolly Parton at the Kennedy Center Awards. Although the audience included such notables as President George W. Bush and entertainment icons Tom Hanks and Steven Spielberg, Jessica blamed the mistake on being nervous about performing before Parton. She was given a chance to rerecord the song for the televised airing of the show, but she was still not satisfied with her performance and producers agreed to cut it from the show.

New Love for Jessica

As her divorce proceedings were still going on, Jessica admitted being upset when news emerged that Nick had started a serious relationship with MTV personality Vanessa Minnillo. "Oh, it hurt me," she told *Elle* magazine in March 2006. In the same interview, Jessica also discussed her reluctance to speak with the media about her divorce:

> "[On *Newlyweds*] I let people [see] who I am and how I react to my husband.... That's a big deal. Celebrities don't do that. So I think [the media] brought me down just because I stopped talking and because I have not spoken—and will not speak—about my divorce. And I think people feel like I owe them my reality right now."

The constant speculation about her private life during her marriage and divorce has taught Jessica to keep a lower profile. During the fall of 2006, tabloids reported that she was "wildly in love" with singer/songwriter John Mayer. Both John and Jessica declined to speak about their relationship, but she did join him while he was on tour during the holiday season.

Photos of the two walking hand-in-hand during John's tour, and pictures of them together on vacation in Rome during early 2007, appeared regularly in celebrity magazines. (As a gag gift to poke fun at the constant media attention, John presented Jessica with a framed cover of one gossip magazine, which featured a headline reading "John Dumps Jessica!")

What the Future Holds for Jessica

During the fall of 2006 Jessica worked on her third feature film, titled *Blonde Ambition*. She plays a young woman who starts at the bottom of a major corporation and works her way up to the top. (The story is loosely based on the 1988 hit *Working Girl*.) *Blonde Ambition*, which also stars comic actor Luke Wilson, was released in 2007. Jessica's fourth movie, *The Witness*, was filmed in early 2007 and was scheduled for release in November of that year.

Although her film career appears to be taking off, Jessica has not neglected her singing. She recently collaborated with her boyfriend John Mayer and rapper Kanye West on the song "Bittersweet" for West's 2007 album *Graduation*. Rumors have also circulated that Jessica and John will sing together on her next album, which is due to be released in 2007.

The singer is also working on her second book, which is titled *Look Up to the Sky*. It will feature her personal journal entries and photography. Her first book, *I Do: Achieving Your Dream Wedding*, was released in 2004.

Lessons Learned 51

"A Public Affair," the first single from Jessica's fourth album, became one of her most popular hits. At one point in July 2006 both "A Public Affair" and Ashlee's song "Invisible" were among the top 10 most downloaded songs on the iTunes Music Store, the first time siblings had accomplished this feat.

ASHLEE AND JESSICA SIMPSON

Jessica chats with VJ Damien Fahey during an appearance on MTV's *Total Request Live*, July 2006. She was excited to begin working on the film *Blonde Ambition*. "I've never had the leading role, and with this one it's really going to be nice to just dive in and kinda wrap my arms around it," she told *Empire Movie News*.

Jessica is also expanding her reach outside of the entertainment world. She launched her own line of hair and beauty products, which are sold on the Home Shopping Network. In 2007 she continued to develop the line.

Giving Back

Jessica also plans to continue her charitable work. One organization that she has become involved in is Operation Smile, which provides surgery to repair children's cleft palates and other facial deformities in

Lessons Learned 53

third-world countries. Jessica has been the organization's International Youth Ambassador since 2003, and in 2005 she traveled to Kenya to visit with more than 280 children who had the life-changing surgery.

The young singer has also been involved with the United Service Organizations (USO), a nonprofit organization that provides entertainment to American soldiers stationed around the world. Jessica has performed for U.S. troops in Pakistan, Afghanistan, Oman, Germany,

Jessica's charitable work has included serving as an International Youth Ambassador for Operation Smile, a nonprofit organization that provides free reconstructive surgery and health care to children around the world who are suffering from facial deformities. Here, she arrives at a news conference on Capitol Hill to discuss the organization and its activities.

ASHLEE AND JESSICA SIMPSON

and Iraq. She has also visited American sailors on their ships and toured military bases in the United States.

In the summer of 2006, when she won a luxury sportscar at the MTV Video Music Awards, she traded the vehicle in for a minivan and then donated the car to the Elim Orphanage. She had previously visited the orphanage with members of her church while a teenager. Jessica also expressed an interest in one day adopting a child.

Ashlee performs during her successful L.O.V.E. Tour in support of *I Am Me*. According to reports in early 2007, a number of stars had expressed an interest in working with Ashlee on her third album, including Tom Petty, Robert Smith of the Cure, Pharrell Williams, India Arie, Timbaland, and John Legend. The album is tentatively scheduled for release late in 2007.

What's Next for Ashlee

Like Jessica, Ashlee has been able to bounce back from controversy. In 2006 MTV's *Total Request Live* named her the Bounce Back Artist of the Year, and she was featured in such magazines as *Elle*, *Cosmopolitan*, *Jane*, *Teen People* (which named her one of its "25 Hottest Stars Under 25" in its June/July issue), and *Blender*, which named her one of the Hottest Women in Pop/R&B in January 2007.

After releasing her second hit album, and embarking on the highly successful L.O.V.E. Tour to support the record, Ashlee returned to her acting roots. She spent the fall of 2006 playing Roxie Hart in the London production of the musical *Chicago*. Her performance was met with solid reviews, with one London critic going calling it "dazzling and near flawless."

Ashlee remains a favorite target of the paparazzi, as is shown by the numerous pictures of her out on the town with various celebrities and musicians. In 2006 she was linked romantically to her band's guitarist, Braxton Olita, and later she was seen with Pete Wentz of the emo band Fall Out Boy. However, both Ashlee and Pete denied that the two had a relationship.

Work is underway on Ashlee's third album, which is expected to be released in the fall of 2007. She has collaborated with a number of talented musicians and producers, including Timbaland, John Legend, Tom Petty, Will.I.Am of Black Eyed Peas, and Pharrell Williams.

Like Jessica, Ashlee continues to do charity work. She is involved with Keep a Child Alive, a nonprofit organization that provides medicines to children infected with AIDS in Africa and other parts of the developing world.

It is clear that both Jessica and Ashlee Simpson have put the controversies of the past behind them. As many new opportunities appear on the horizon, the Simpson sisters are poised to maintain their positions at the top of the entertainment world for many years to come.

CHRONOLOGY

1980 Jessica Ann Simpson is born on July 10.

1984 Ashlee Nicole Simpson is born on October 3.

1992 Jessica auditions unsuccessfully for the Disney variety show *The All-New Mickey Mouse Club*.

1995 Ashlee becomes the youngest student admitted to the School of American Ballet in New York City. While there, she battles problems with the eating disorder anorexia nervosa.

1999 Tommy Mottola signs Jessica to Columbia Records.

After the success of her first single, "I Wanna Love You Forever," Jessica's album *Sweet Kisses* is released.

She begins dating Nick Lachey of 98 Degrees.

2000 Jessica performs at a Christmas special in Washington, D.C.

2001 Jessica performs at the inauguration of President George W. Bush.

Ashlee gets a small role on the popular television program *Malcolm in the Middle*.

2002 Jessica is named number one on *Maxim* magazine's fifth annual Hot 100 List.

In February, Nick and Jessica become engaged, and they marry in October.

Ashlee has a small part in the film *The Hot Chick*, and also gets a recurring role on the television drama *7th Heaven*.

2003 In August, *Newlyweds: Nick and Jessica* airs on MTV, and immediately becomes a huge hit.

Jessica's fourth album, *In This Skin*, is released; it eventually sells over 4 million copies.

Ashlee contributes a song to the soundtrack of the film *Freaky Friday*.

2004 *The Nick and Jessica Variety Hour* airs on television.

CHRONOLOGY

The *Ashlee Simpson Show* gives viewers an intimate glimpse into Ashlee's personal life, documenting the making of her first album.

Autobiography is released in July and debuts in the top spot on the Billboard chart.

Ashlee's appearance on *Saturday Night Live*, in which she is shown to be singing along with prerecorded vocals, causes great controversy.

Jessica releases *Rejoyce: The Christmas Album* in time for the holiday season.

2005 The last episode of *Newlyweds* airs on March 30.

Jessica stars in the hit film *The Dukes of Hazzard*, which earns more than $110 million.

In November Nick and Jessica decide to separate.

Ashlee releases her second album, *I Am Me*, in October and embarks on a successful tour to promote the record.

2006 Nick and Jessica's divorce is finalized on July 20.

Jessica stars in the film *Employee of the Month*.

Her album *A Public Affair* is released by Epic Records.

She begins dating singer John Mayer.

Ashlee draws good reviews for her performance as Roxie Hart in the London production of the musical *Chicago*.

2007 Jessica's film *Blonde Ambition*, also starring Luke Wilson, is released.

Ashlee releases her third album.

ACCOMPLISHMENTS & AWARDS

Jessica Simpson

Albums
- **1999** *Sweet Kisses*
- **2001** *Irresistible*
- **2002** *This Is the Remix*
- **2003** *In This Skin*
- **2004** *Rejoyce: The Christmas Album*
- **2006** *A Public Affair*

Films
- **2002** *The Master of Disguise*
- **2005** *The Dukes of Hazzard*
- **2006** *Employee of the Month*
- **2007** *The Witness*
- *Blonde Ambition*

Television shows
- **2004** *The Nick and Jessica Variety Hour*
- **2003–05** *Newlyweds: Nick & Jessica*

Awards
- **2000** Winner, Teen Choice Award for Choice Breakout Artist and Love Song of the Year (for "Where You Are")
- **2004** Nominated, Teen Choice Award for Choice TV Personality (Female),

    Winner, Teen Choice Award for Choice Reality/Variety TV Star (Female)
- **2005** Winner, Teen Choice Award for Choice TV Personality (Female)
- **2006** Nominated, MTV Movie Award for Best On-Screen Team for *The Dukes of Hazzard* (with Johnny Knoxville and Sean William Scott)

    Nominated, MTV Movie Award for Sexiest Performance for *The Dukes of Hazzard*

    Nominated, People's Choice Award for Favorite Song from a Movie, for "These Boots are Made for Walkin'"

    Winner, Teen Choice Award for Choice Breakout (Female) for *The Dukes of Hazzard*

    Nominated, Teen Choice Award for Choice Hottie (Female) and Choice Female Red Carpet Fashion Icon

ACCOMPLISHMENTS & AWARDS

Ashlee Simpson

Albums
- **2004** *Autobiography*
- **2005** *I Am Me*

Films
- **2002** *The Hot Chick*
- **2005** *Undiscovered*

Television Shows
- **2001** *Malcolm in the Middle* (guest appearance)
- **2002–3** *7th Heaven*
- **2004–5** *The Ashlee Simpson Show*

Awards
- **2003** Nominated, Teen Choice Award for Choice TV Breakout Star (Female) for *7th Heaven*

- **2004** Winner, Teen Choice Awards for Choice Fresh Face and Choice Song of the Summer (for "Pieces of Me")

    Winner, Billboard Music Award for Female New Artist of the Year

- **2005** Nominated, World Music Awards for World's Best Selling New Female Artist and World's Best Selling Pop/Rock Artist

    Nominated, MTV Video Music Award for Best Pop Video for "Pieces of Me"

    Nominated, Groovevolt Music and Fashion Award for Best Song Performance—Female for "Pieces Of Me"

    Nominated, Teen Choice Award for Choice TV Personality (Female)

- **2006** Winner, MTV Total Request Live Bounce Back Artist of the Year

    Winner, MTV Australia Video Music Awards for Best Female Artist and Best Pop Video (for "Boyfriend")

FURTHER READING & INTERNET RESOURCES

Books

Adams, Michelle. *Jessica Simpson.* Hockessin, Del.: Mitchell Lane, 2007.

Casapulla, Louise. *Ashlee Simpson.* New York: Scholastic, 2005.

Dougherty, Terri. *People in the News: Jessica Simpson and Nick Lachey.* San Diego: Lucent Books, 2005.

Kjelle, Marylou Morano. *Ashlee Simpson.* Hockessin, Del.: Mitchell Lane, 2005.

Norwich, Grace. *Ashlee Simpson: Out of the Shadow and into the Spotlight.* New York: Simon Spotlight, 2005.

Wheeler, Jill. *Jessica Simpson.* Edina, Minn.: Checkerboard Books, 2004.

Web Sites

www.ashleesimpsonmusic.com/
Ashlee Simpson keeps in touch with her fans on a regular basis as she posts blogs on her Web site telling about her next career moves.

www.epicrecords.com/
Information about Jessica Simpson is available at the Web site of her record label, Epic Records.

www.geffen.com/
Visit the Web site of Ashlee Simpson's record label, Geffen Records, for information about her upcoming releases.

www.jessicasimpson.com/
Jessica Simpson's fans can follow what she's doing next on her homepage, which includes information about her upcoming movies, record releases, and other professional and personal news.

www.myspace.com/jessicasimpson
www.myspace.com/ashleesimpson
Jessica's and Ashlee's friends can keep up with their latest news on their MySpace pages.

www.operationsmile.org/aboutus/spokespeople/jessica_simpson
Learn about Jessica Simpson's work for Operation Smile as she travels the world in support of Operation Smile.

GLOSSARY

acid reflux disease—also called gastroesophageal reflux disease (GERD), is is chronic symptoms or mucosal damage produced by the abnormal reflux of gastric contents into the esophagus

anorexia nervosa—a serious eating disorder that is found primarily among young women in their teens and early twenties. It is characterized by a pathological fear of weight gain, which leads to faulty eating patterns, malnutrition, and excessive weight loss.

aspiration—a strong desire to achieve something great or important.

conglomerate—a large business organization that consists of a number of companies that deal with many different commercial activities.

contemporary—something that is distinctly modern in style.

mainstream—reflecting the ideas, actions, and values that are most widely accepted by a group or society.

malapropism—the misuse of a word through confusion with another word that sounds similar but is ludicrously wrong in the context.

niche—a place or activity that particularly suits somebody's talents and personality.

paparazzi—freelance photographers who aggressively pursue celebrities for the purpose of taking candid photographs which can be sold to tabloid newspapers and gossip magazines; the singular is *paparazzo*.

perseverance—steady and continued action or belief, usually over a long period; steadfastness.

platinum—a recording-industry designation given to a record that sells more than a million copies.

reality television—a genre of programming that presents purportedly unscripted dramatic or humorous situations, documents actual events, and features ordinary people instead of professional actors.

secular—not overtly or specifically religious.

unscripted—not following a prepared script.

INDEX

Aissa, Rod, 29
The All-New Mickey Mouse Club, 14
anorexia nervosa, 16, 46
Applegate, Christina, 49
The Ashlee Simpson Show, 30–31, 36
Autobiography (Ashlee Simpson), 10, 31–33, 36, 38

Billboard Music Awards, 38
Blonde Ambition (film), 50, 52

Cabrera, Ryan, 31, 33
charity work
  Ashlee Simpson, 55
  Jessica Simpson, 52–54
childhood and family life, 12–16
Cook, Dane, 49

Davis, Clive, 30
Dick, Andy, 49
Drew, Tina Ann. *See* Simpson, Tina (mother)
The Dukes of Hazzard, 12, 40–41, 43
Dupri, Jermaine, 30
Durst, Fred, 43
Dykstra, Katherine, 8, 10

Employee of the Month (film), 49

Fahey, Damien, 52

Henderson, Josh, 31, 33
Hilton, Paris, 48

I Am Me (Ashlee Simpson), 38, 39, 46, 54
I Do: Achieving Your Dream Wedding (book), 25, 50
In This Skin (Jessica Simpson), 8, 28
Irresistible (Jessica Simpson), 18–19

Jackson, Janet, 30
Jones, Kimberly, 47

Keep a Child Alive, 55
Knoxville, Johnny, 41, 43

Lachey, Drew, 29
Lachey, Nick, 8–10, 12, 18, 22–30, 36, 39–40, 42–43, 49
Levine, Adam, 43
Lohan, Lindsay, 46, 48
Longoria, Eva, 49
Look Up to the Sky (book), 50

Margera, Bam, 43
Maxim, 21
Mayer, John, 50
Minnillo, Vanessa, 49
Mottola, Tommy, 16–17
MTV, 8, 9, 24, 27–28, 30, 37, 41, 52

Newlyweds: Nick and Jessica, 8–10, 22–25, 27–30, 39–40, 50
The Nick and Jessica Variety Hour, 28
98 Degrees, 8–9, 18, 24, 27
  See also Lachey, Nick

Olita, Braxton, 55
Operation Smile, 52–53

Parton, Dolly, 49
People's Choice Awards, 8
A Public Affair (Jessica Simpson), 47, 49, 51

Rejoyce: The Christmas Album (Jessica Simpson), 28

Saturday Night Live, 36–39
School of American Ballet, 8, 15–16
Scott, Seann William, 41

INDEX

Seacrest, Ryan, 49
7th Heaven, 8, 20, 21
Shepard, Dax, 49
Simpson, Ashlee
  acting career, 8, 20, 21, 29–30, 45, 47, 55
  and anorexia nervosa, 16, 46
  on *The Ashlee Simpson Show*, 30–31, 36
  awards won by, 8, 38, 55
  birth and childhood, 12–16
  charity work of, 55
  cosmetic surgery of, 46
  critical reception of, 32, 33, 47, 55
  feud of, with Lindsay Lohan, 46, 48
  friendship of, with Jessica, 11, 14–15, 44–45
  lip-synchs on *Saturday Night Live*, 36–39
  music career, 10, 21, 28, 31–33, 38–39, 54–55
  and the paparazzi, 7–8, 11, 35–36, 55
  romantic relationships, 31, 55
  at the School of American Ballet, 8, 15–16
  on *7th Heaven*, 8, 20, 21
Simpson, Jessica
  acting career, 40–41, 49, 50
  awards won by, 8, 18, 40–41
  birth and childhood, 12–16
  books written by, 25, 50
  charity work of, 52–54
  Christian music career, 8, 14, 16
  critical reception of, 40, 49
  divorce of, from Nick Lachey, 42–43
  and the Dolly Parton tribute, 49
  friendship of, with Ashlee, 11, 14–15, 44–45
  and grandmother Joyce, 8, 16, 28
  marriage of, to Nick Lachey, 24–27, 36, 39–40
  music career, 16–19, 21, 28, 46–47, 49, 50–51
  on *Newlyweds*, 8–10, 22–25, 27–30, 39–40, 50
  and the paparazzi, 7–8, 11, 35–36
  romantic relationships, 50
Simpson, Joe (father), 8, 12–14, 16, 27, 40
Simpson, Tina (mother), 8, 12–14
Sweet Kisses (Jessica Simpson), 18, 19

Taylor, Chuck, 49
Teen Choice Awards, 8, 18, 40–41
This Is the Remix (Jessica Simpson), 21
Total Request Live, 37

Undiscovered (film), 45, 47
United Service Organizations (USO), 53–54

Valderrama, Wilmer, 46

Wentz, Pete, 55
West, Kanye, 50
Wilson, Luke, 50

ABOUT THE AUTHORS

Kristy Kaminsky is an editorial assistant for a non-profit association in Princeton, New Jersey. She enjoys spending summers in the sun along the Jersey Shore listening to Jimmy Buffett albums, and is currently planning her wedding for the fall of 2008. She loves spending time with Brian, her incredible intelligent fiancé. Kristy dedicates this book to her supportive parents, David and Barbara.

Brian Domboski is a commercial banker by trade, but also keeps an ever-vigilant eye on the world of celebrity gossip. He is an avid Philadelphia Phillies and Eagles fan and enjoys spending time with his amazing fiancée, Kristy, and his adoring cat, Abigail. His true passions include a rousing game of softball, a platter of sushi, and listening to Tupac Shakur and Modest Mouse albums. Brian credits his parents, Rick and Patty, for inspiring him to write, and dedicates this book to his sister Kristen, currently serving with the U.S. Army Reserves in Kosovo.

Picture Credits

page

- **2:** Michael Caulfield/WireImage
- **6:** Newswire Photo Service/NMI
- **9:** MTV/FPS
- **10:** Geffen Records/KRT
- **12:** Kathy Hutchins/Hutchins Photo
- **15:** WENN Archive
- **17:** WirePix/FPS
- **19:** Columbia Records/NMI
- **20:** Geffen Records/FPS
- **22:** MTV/News Photo Services
- **25:** Chicken of the Sea/FPS
- **26:** New Millennium Images
- **29:** kgku-24/INF/Goff
- **30:** RCA Music Group/NMI
- **31:** Geffen Records/FPS
- **32:** New Millennium Images
- **34:** Ace Pictures
- **37:** KRT/MCT
- **38:** New Millennium Images
- **41:** Warner Bros./NMI
- **42:** New Millennium Images
- **44:** Kevin Mazur/WireImage
- **47:** Lions Gate Films/NMI
- **48:** Abaca Press/KRT
- **51:** Ai Wire Photos
- **52:** FilmMagic
- **53:** Roll Call Photos
- **54:** AdMedia/Sipa Press

Front cover: DD1/ZOB/WENN
Back cover: Ace Pictures